Young Blackbeard

by

Michael Lawrence

Illustrated by Donough O'Malley

First published in 2010 in Great Britain by
Barrington Stoke Ltd
18 Walker St, Edinburgh, EH3 7LP

www.barringtonstoke.co.uk

ISBN: 978-1-84299-769-7

Printed in Great Britain by Bell & Bain Ltd

AUTHOR ID

Name: Michael Lawrence

Likes: Bananas.

Dislikes: CCTV cameras.

3 words that best describe me:
Swashbuckling parrot fancier.

A secret not many people know:
I have a full-sized suit of armour and collect swords and shields.

ILLUSTRATOR ID

Name: Donough O'Malley

Likes: Cheese, rock & roll, roast dinners, drawing, kites, pandas, reading, badminton, Saturday mornings lying in bed, movies, South America and hanging out with my mates!

Dislikes: Rude loud people, celery, soppy love songs, the flu and exams!

3 words that best describe me: Tall, silly, Irish.

A secret not many people know:
I fart a lot when I eat vegetable soup. Don't tell anyone!

Contents

Chapter 1
Cabin Boy

There was once a bold and terrible pirate known as Blackbeard, who was feared across the Caribbean. He is said to have taken fourteen wives, shot his first mate to make his crew fear him, and forced some of his captives to eat their own ears. Nasty stuff, but whoever heard of a nice pirate?

Blackbeard wasn't his real name, of course. At the time of his birth and for some years afterwards he did not have a beard of

any colour, so calling him Blackbeard wouldn't have been very bright. His true name was Edward Teach.

Teach was born in Bristol in the 1680s. Very little is known about his childhood other than that he went to sea at an early age, but as it happens, I know something about Young Blackbeard that you won't find in any history books, or even on the Internet. How? Because my next-door-neighbour has an old sea chest that's been passed down in his family. A chest that once belonged to Blackbeard the Pirate's half-sister Mildred. And it contains documents that tell of the infamous pirate's early days at sea.

This is the story of one of those adventures.

Have you ever been sick? I don't mean unwell, or off school, or anything as ordinary as that. I mean sick-sick. Throwing-up sick.

Hanging-over-the-toilet sick and thinking there can't possibly be any more sick inside you. Well, that's the kind of sick young Edward Teach was on his third sea voyage with the famous pirate Henry Honeycombe on his ship *The Salty Blighter*.

You see, Edward hadn't yet got what's called his 'sea legs'. When you have your sea legs you can stand upright on deck and not rush to the side of the ship every time it rises on a wave. Oh, how the pirates laughed when Edward did that!

Edward Teach was the ship's cabin boy. The cabin boy's job was to clear up after the men. He also had to organise the rum breaks and wash up. It wasn't a great job, but it was what every cabin boy did on a pirate ship.

It was a Pirate Rule that a boy must do four sea voyages before he could become a deck boy. Deck boys didn't have to bring the rum or wipe the plates. They had to clear up the huge piles of vomit the pirates spewed because they drank too much rum. Edward looked forward to the day he became a deck boy.

You might be interested to hear some other Pirate Rules. Here are four of them.

1. Everyone on a pirate ship has to look like a pirate at all times and say 'Ah-harr' and 'Avast, ye swabs,' at least once a day.

2. Every morning, before breakfast, a pirate must spit at the ship's flag (the Skull and Crossbones) and beat his chest like a gorilla.

3. No pirate can change his clothes or wash during a voyage.

4. If any ships are spotted on the horizon they must be chased and boarded.

5. Boarded ships must be sunk as soon as everyone on them is either killed, put in a leaky boat far from land, or made to walk the plank over a shark.

(Yes, I know that's five Rules, and you know it's five Rules, but pirates cannot count that high.)

Edward sometimes wished his grown-up shipmates weren't so unkind to everyone, but he knew that if he said such a thing he would be thrown over the side before he could say 'Hey, I'm sorry, all right?' He couldn't afford to lose this job. There was so little work back in Bristol for someone as young as he, with no education and bad teeth.

OK, that's the background. Now let's get to the story. Next chapter.

Chapter 2
Foggy Island

One morning, the crew of *The Salty Blighter* woke to find that they had entered a fog so thick and dark that nothing could be seen in any direction. The captain ordered the sails to be lowered so the ship would come to a stop.

"Too risky to go on blindly," he said. "Might be another ship in this fog and we don't want to bump into it."

The men settled down to wait for the fog to clear. For all that day and the following night they waited, but when they woke on the second morning it was as thick as ever.

"The fog might never lift," the first mate said to the captain. "We might be sitting here till the flesh drops off our bones."

The first mate's name was Tobias Tobias, but he liked to be called TT because Tobias Tobias was such a stupid name. The captain thought over TT's words.

"Very well," said he. "We'll go on."

So the sails were raised again, and a small breeze filled them, and the ship moved forward – but not far, for almost at once there was a grinding sound and the vessel shuddered to a stop. *The Salty Blighter* had struck rocks in the shallow waters of an island.

"You idiot!" the captain said, slapping his mate's left ear. The reason he slapped TT's left ear was that he'd lost his right one years ago. (Pretty careless, you might think, but it wasn't his fault. He lost it in a fight with one of his ex-wives. She bit it off.)

As it happened, TT wasn't wrong about the fog not lifting. Fog clung to this island like chewing gum to the sole of a 21st-century shoe. It never went away, whatever the month or weather. Strong sunlight couldn't break through it, high temperatures couldn't dissolve it, strong winds couldn't huff it away, heavy rains couldn't soak through it.

But covered in fog or not, an island was an island and the crew had been at sea for a long time. They'd been looking forward to walking on dry land again, and here it was. It was the thought of this that caused one of the men standing on the foggy deck to say something.

"How about an extra tot of rum all round as we've reached dry land, Captain?"

The captain peered through the fog. "Who said that?" he growled.

The man who had spoken gulped. When the captain growled it was impossible to tell what sort of mood he was in. Sometimes his growl was followed by a laugh. Other times it was followed by an order to give a man twenty lashes with the cat-o'-nine-tails or hang him by his big toes from the yard-arm. So the pirate stepped further back into the fog and put someone else in front of him: young Edward Teach.

"It was the boy," the man said.

"It didn't sound like him," the captain said.

"I think his voice is breaking," the man replied. He leaned close to Edward. "Say it was you or you're in trouble," he whispered.

"Boy!" the captain said fiercely. "Here, where I can see you!"

Edward stepped forward. "Y-yes, C-Captain?"

"It was your idea that I give every man on board an extra round of rum because we hit dry land?"

"Um ... yes, Captain. Sorry, bad idea."

The captain threw back his head and roared – with laughter.

"Bad idea? Not at all. Brilliant idea! TT, get the rum out!"

A cheer went up on the deck of *The Salty Blighter*, and all but one of the crew slapped

Edward on the back. (His back was black and blue by the time they'd finished.)

Edward didn't take any rum himself. It wasn't because he was too young, it was simply that he didn't like the stuff. But everyone on a pirate ship was expected to like rum. The men laughed at the faces he pulled whenever he tasted it.

"Soft kid!" they said.

"Can't take his drink!" they guffawed.

"He'll never make a pirate!" they jeered.

No one else gave the rum a miss the day they landed on Foggy Island, and it went down so well that the captain ordered the men to carry a barrel ashore. They did so, cheerfully.

Now rum is a very warming drink, and as it was even colder on the island than it had been on the ship, more of it was passed around, and soon Edward was the only one still shivering.

"Captain," he said. "Permission to go and find some firewood."

"Go ahead, lad!" the captain said. The rum had put him in a very jolly mood.

So, while the crew carried on drinking, young Edward set off into the thick fog to search for wood to make a fire.

Chapter 3
Beware! Ghosts!

Now the trouble with fog is that you never know what your next step will take you to. It might, for example, take you to a fist that's waiting there to flatten your nose, or over the edge of a pit filled with poisonous snakes. Neither of these things happened to Edward, but the fog made him very nervous. So nervous indeed that when he crashed into something hard enough to be a brick wall his heart almost leapt out of his mouth. Once he'd calmed down he peered at the thing he'd crashed into and saw that it was a huge rock. He also saw that words had been scratched into the rock. These words:

Beware! Ghosts!

A shiver of fear went through Edward. Ghosts? The fog was bad enough, but ... ghosts? Did he really want to go further into haunted fog? He cleared his throat and called out, very softly.

"Hello? Is there anybody there?"

He rather hoped there'd be no reply to his question, but out of the dense dark fog came a very odd voice.

"Don't drink the water," the odd voice said. And then again: "Don't drink the water."

This voice, coming all unseen out of the fog, made Edward gulp. So much did the unseen voice make him gulp, in fact, that he

thought he might grope his way back to the beach with as much speed as the fog would allow. He was about to start this hasty return when he remembered that his crew-mates were always saying that he would never make a pirate, and instead clenched his fists, and stayed where he was.

"Who's there?" he said as boldly as he could. "Are you a ... ghost?"

"You could say that, you could say that," answered the foggy voice.

Edward now called up all his courage and felt his way round the rock with the awful message.

"Where are you?" he asked.

This time there was no reply, which was almost as scary as there being one. But Edward stepped further into the fog, with his hands stretched out in front of him. When his

front foot touched something that went
clatter-clatter-click-click-clunk he stopped
suddenly – well, wouldn't you? – and,
stooping, felt around for whatever it was that
had made such an odd sound.

He touched something thin and smooth. Then he touched another something, very like the first, then another, and another, each one as round and smooth as a fat chopstick. He also felt some sort of material that seemed to be attached to the twig-like objects, but thought nothing of this for the moment. He was just thinking that he might have found his firewood when the fog lifted a little and he saw what it really was that he was touching and fell backwards in horror.

The bones of a human skeleton!

He was still sitting on the ground, gasping with shock, when the fog shifted a bit more and he saw that there was more than one skeleton. Many more. Most were human, but there were also the skeletons of a number of animals with black hair on what was left of their backs.

"Goats?" said Edward aloud, and quite rightly.

He had just noticed that one of the human skeletons wore a cloak made of the same hair – a goat-skin cloak – when the odd voice came again out of the fog.

"Don't drink the water, don't drink the water," it said.

Edward looked about him. Had the voice come from one of the skeletons? Would all of them sit up and stare at him? This was too much, even for someone who wanted to be a pirate. He started to get to his feet, to make a run for it.

He had got as far as his knees when something did indeed move among the skeletons. It came from the shoulder of the one in the hairy black cloak. But it wasn't part of that skeleton. No, it was a separate skeleton. A very small one, which hopped towards him. Edward panicked.

"Get away from me! Don't touch me!"

In his haste to escape the small assortment of bones, he fell sideways – into a pool of water. He scrambled to his feet and would have jumped out and raced into the fog, careless of what he might bump into, but the little skeleton now stood on the bank of the pool, staring at him with the black holes of its tiny skull.

"Don't drink the water," it said in its odd voice. "Don't drink the water."

Chapter 4
A Pirate Parrot's Tale

Edward was surprised to hear these words coming from the little skeleton.

"It was you!" he cried.

"It was, it was, it is, it is," was the bony reply. "Don't drink the water, don't drink the water."

Edward looked down at the pond he was standing in. "This water?"

"Any water, any water, it's poisoned, poisoned."

"And those skeletons over there ..."

"They drank it, they drank it. It killed 'em, killed 'em."

Edward waded out of the water. "Well, thanks for the warning."

"You're welcome, welcome."

He frowned. "Why do you say everything twice?"

"I'm a parrot," snapped the bony creature. "It's what parrots do."

"You didn't say that twice."

"I forgot, I forgot."

"Well seeing as you're an ex-parrot, not a flesh and feathers one, how about forgetting totally?"

"I thought humans liked the way parrots talked," said the parrot.

"Not this human," said Edward.

"I'll just shut up then, shall I?"

"No, you don't have to do that. Just say everything once, that's all."

"All right then," said the parrot. "To tell you the truth, saying everything twice all the time drives me nuts."

"Who did all these skeletons belong to?" Edward asked the parrot.

"The human ones belonged to pirates," the featherless bird explained. "The one in the goat-skin was the captain. Captain

Crooke. Our ship was smashed to pieces in a storm one night long ago."

"Do you think the captain would mind if I borrowed his cloak? It's a bit nippy here."

"I think that if he could get up he'd turn you inside out and eat your kidneys for breakfast," said the parrot. "But as he can't, go ahead."

Edward undid the goat-skin cloak from the captain's skeleton and wrapped it round himself. At once, he felt warmer. Then he asked the parrot if it knew where he could find some wood for a fire. The parrot said that it did and hopped away. When Edward didn't follow right away the parrot spoke again, from the depths of the fog.

"Do you want firewood or don't you?"

Edward went after the parrot. He couldn't see it, or where they were going, so every now and then he called out. The parrot replied each time, and after a while Edward stepped out into a small dip in the land. The fog was a little thinner here, so he could just make out the parrot waiting for him by the remains of a long-dead fire. There was a lot of unburnt wood around the fire. There was also a lot of black goats' hair.

"Before the island's goats were poisoned most of their hair fell out," the parrot said when he asked about this.

Edward picked up a clump of the hair. It reminded him of the ragged beard of the ship's carpenter, Inky Klebbs. He had always wished he could grow a beard like Inky's. He couldn't, yet, but here was his chance to see how such a beard might feel. He gathered some more clumps of hair and knotted them together. Then he tied the hairy mass about his ears and made a space for his mouth. There was another pond nearby, and he bent over it and peered at himself. He was quite pleased with what he saw.

"All you need is a pair of horns and you'd frighten yourself," the parrot said.

"Horns?" said Edward.

The parrot hopped to a skeleton Edward hadn't noticed. Another goat's skeleton. He joined the parrot, picked up the skeleton's horned skull and put it on top of his head like a hat.

"Too small," he said. "It'll fall off if I move."

"Tie it on then, like you did the beard," said the parrot.

Edward took some more strands of goat hair and tied the skull onto his head, with a knot under his chin. Then he leant over the water again.

"You look a bit like my captain when he was alive," the parrot said.

"Did he wear horns too, then?"

"No. But he looked pretty horrible."

Edward was thrilled to hear that he looked like a dead pirate. He might still be a cabin boy, but now that he'd learnt how to look like a pirate, well, maybe he would be one some day, after all!

Chapter 5
Treasure Trove

Now Edward began to wonder what had poisoned the water that had killed the pirates and the goats, and this is what the parrot told him.

When the storm drove Captain Crooke's ship onto the rocks all those years ago most of the crew were drowned, but a few, including the captain, were washed up onto the shore. (The parrot had flown there, of course.) Because their ship was wrecked, they couldn't get off the island, and because the fog never lifted, they didn't know if there was any food there – apart for the goats, which were everywhere.

"Goats and fish, that's all there was to eat," the parrot said.

One day, when flying around in the fog to stretch its wings, the parrot had come upon the crew of another pirate ship that had run aground, but on the other side of the island. This crew were fighting among themselves over some treasure they'd come to bury.

Edward's eyes flared like small torches at the sound of this. "Treasure?" he said. "I've never seen any treasure. Not much anyway. When we board a ship there's never anything worth having, somehow. I've always dreamed of finding *real* treasure!"

The parrot went on with its tale. "Most of the pirates had been killed by their shipmates. The few that were left had just finished burying the treasure when one of them, who'd gone off to look for food, returned to say that he'd seen our camp. The pirates didn't want to risk their treasure being found, so they decided to poison the island's water before leaving. This they did, and next day my captain and his men drank the water and died. A day or two later the goats died too, but not before most of their hair had fallen out."

"And you?" said Edward.

"I didn't drink the water," the parrot said. "I'd heard the pirates talk of poisoning it. I might be a parrot, but I'm not bird-brained. I told my captain 'Don't drink the water,' I said, 'don't drink the water,' but he didn't listen."

"Why not?"

"Pirates don't listen to parrots. They just strut about with them on their shoulders trying to teach them to say funny things. It's quite insulting really."

"I don't understand," Edward said. "How is it that you're a skeleton if you didn't drink the water?"

"I died of thirst," answered the parrot.

"Oh. Sorry to hear that."

"Forget it. It was a long time ago."

"Was it the pirates with the treasure who wrote the message on the rock back there?"

"What message?"

"*Beware! Ghosts!*"

"Oh, that. Yes. They hoped to scare people off so they wouldn't find the treasure. Would you like to see it?"

"See what?"

"The treasure, the treasure," replied the parrot.

"You weren't going to do that again," said Edward.

"I wasn't doing it again, I was just trying to hurry things along. Do you want to see it or not?"

"The treasure's still here?"

"Yes. It's being dug up as we speak."

"Dug up? Who by?"

"Three of the men who put it in the ground all those years ago have come back for it."

"There are other pirates on this island right now?" Edward blurted with some alarm.

"Didn't I just say so?" said the parrot.

"Well, yes, but …"

Edward was still getting over this when an enormous seagull swooped out of the fog and drank from the pond he and the parrot were sitting beside.

"Don't drink the water," the parrot said to the seagull.

The seagull looked at the parrot as if it were crazy, cackled with laughter, drank from the pond, and flew back up into the fog.

"The poison must have worn off," said
Edward.

There was a rush of wings followed by a
splash. The seagull had fallen out of the fog
and landed in the water. And there it stayed,
floating on its back, quite still.

"Or maybe not," said Edward.

"Do you want to see the treasure?" the
parrot asked him.

"Well, I *do*, but what about the men
who've come for it?"

The parrot put its head to one side and
gave him a look of pity. "For someone in a
beard like that you ought to be more bold
than you are," it said.

"I was only asking," said Edward. "I do
want to see the treasure, really I do. Lead on,
parrot!"

The parrot hopped into the fog and Edward went after it once again. Soon they were climbing a rocky hill of some sort. Feeling his way very carefully, Edward was glad the parrot was just ahead of him, the sound of its bony wings rattling let him know which way to go. At the top of the hill, the parrot stopped and hopped onto his shoulder.

"They're down there," it said.

"Who are?"

"The pirates digging up their treasure."

"I can't see a thing," said Edward.

This was very true, for the fog was thicker than ever up there. Among the things he couldn't see were all the loose stones on the side of the hill. Peering down into the fog, Edward leaned out too far and lost his footing, and suddenly he was slipping and sliding, down, down, down, still on his feet but yelling wildly, terrified of where he was going in the swirling mist. The parrot clung to his shoulder as if its life depended on it (which it didn't, of course).

Down below, where the fog was thinner, the three old men who had just dug up the treasure they and their shipmates buried long ago, jumped in shock. What was that hideous sound from above?

Looking up, the pirates saw a dreadful figure zooming down out of the dense cloud of fog. Bolt upright it stood, arms stretched out, wailing in a high, eerie voice. A great black cloak billowed, and it wore an enormous black beard, and had horns upon its head and the skeleton of a parrot on its shoulder.

It was terrifying!

So terrifying indeed that two of the men clutched their hearts, sank to their knees, and died, at that very instant. The third, whose heart was a little stronger, turned and ran into the fog and all the way to his boat.

What did treasure matter when the devil was on your heels?

Landing in a heap at the foot of the hill, Edward rolled into the pit the men had dug. There he sat up, dazed and confused.

"What happened?" he asked the parrot, who had hopped to the edge of the pit.

"You frightened them to death," said the parrot. "Two of them anyway. The third made a run for it. I doubt we'll be seeing *him* again."

"I frightened them?" Edward said in amazement. He'd never frightened anyone before.

He stared out of the pit at the two men who had died of shock.

"They're very old for pirates," he said.

"They were quite a bit younger when they buried the treasure," the parrot answered. "They might even have been the only three still alive. Down to one now, thanks to you."

Edward climbed out and examined the chest the pirates had dug up. It was locked, but the lock was as old as the pirates themselves and he opened it with a few thumps of a stone. When he lifted the lid and saw the chest's contents he gasped. He was looking at the kind of treasure he'd been dreaming about since he first thought of joining a pirate ship!

Chapter 6
Young Blackbeard

So keen was Edward to get back to the beach and tell the captain about the treasure that he forgot all about collecting firewood. Besides, he wasn't cold any more thanks to the goat-skin cloak. The parrot rode on his shoulder and directed him. It had been on the island for so long that it knew every inch of it in spite of the fog.

Edward didn't know how close he was to the beach when he tripped over an exposed tree root. As he threw his arms out to save himself from falling, the parrot squawked and dug its bony claws into his shoulder. The crew on the beach jumped at the squawk and saw, lurching out of the fog, a ghastly, hairy-cloaked figure with horns and the skeleton of a parrot on its shoulder.

None of the captain's men died of shock, but a few ran into the sea in terror, and those who had been dozing after all the rum they'd drunk, woke with a start and ran around in confused circles thinking they were under attack.

"It's all right, it's only me!" Edward shouted.

He had to repeat this several times before it sank in. Then the pirates came to him and tugged at his beard and inspected the little skeleton on his shoulder. The parrot told them to keep their hands to themselves.

Most of the crew were amused by both the parrot and how Edward looked. They were also very interested when he opened his pockets and took out a string of pearls, a couple of brooches and some gold coins. He told them that this was just part of a treasure that some other pirates had been digging up and that he had scared them off. The captain clapped him on the back.

"Well, Young Blackbeard," he said. "It looks like there's a pirate in you after all!"

These words were music to Edward's ears. Captain Honeycombe told him to lead them to the treasure.

"Can I have a tot of rum first, Cap'n?" Edward asked.

The captain laughed, and handed him a tot. Edward drank it down and did not pull a face. Then he went back into the fog. The

men followed him. (The parrot led the way, of course.)

When they reached the pit and the two pirates who had died of fright, Edward opened the treasure chest. When he opened it earlier the chest had been stuffed with jewels and coins, but now it was just over half full. Still, there was enough left to delight the captain and his men, who carried the chest back to the beach, singing all the way, as pirates do when they've found treasure.

A few days later, when they had pulled *The Salty Blighter* off the rocks and repaired some minor damage, Captain Honeycombe and his crew sailed away from the island.

And there you have it. The story of how Edward Teach learned to scare people and how he was first called by the name that would one day make him feared all across the Caribbean. Some years after his first

visit to Foggy Island, Edward paid a fisherman to take him back there. There, again guided by the parrot (which would stay with him until its old bones crumbled to dust), he found the spot where he had terrified the pirates digging up the treasure. The two who died of fright that day were skeletons themselves now. Their bones marked the spot where Edward had buried the treasure he'd removed from the chest before returning to the beach to tell Captain Honeycombe about it. It had been the parrot's idea to do that. Smart bird!

When he left the island the second time, Edward was quite a wealthy young man. He used his fortune to buy his first proper ship and pay his first proper pirate crew.

And he started to grow his famous beard. His beard was a very ordinary brown, so he dyed it black, like the hair of the goats on Foggy Island. He grew the beard long, and braided it, and tied black ribbons in the ends of the braids, and when attacking a ship he would stuff burning ropes under his big black hat, which made it look as if his head was on fire.

No one – but no one – was ever as scary as Blackbeard the Pirate!

Barrington Stoke would like to thank all its readers for commenting on the manuscript before publication and in particular:

Hamed Awale
Mohamed Awale
Harvey Beament
Ricky Black
Asaph Bondo
Alex Brown
Carly Burns
Saskia Burns
Sophie Curran
Fiona Currie
Thomas Gannicott-Porter
Lianne Gunn
Jake
Marilyn Jones
Trish Jones
Athul Jose
Joanne Kenney
Kieran McNamee
Andrew Muir
Alex Nicolson

Lisa Palmer
Thomas Palmer
Ian-James Perks
Alyson Phillips
Jane Priest
Sancia Sam
Bobby Sarvagode
Joanne Savage
Bridget Smith
Katherine Forrest Smith
Shannon Smith
Siobhan Smith
Nicholas Biju Thomas
Sandi Thornton
Solomon Thornton
George Toone
Jordan Trainer
Tom Val
W. L. Wildridge

Become a Consultant!

Would you like to be a consultant? Ask your parent, carer or teacher to contact us at the email address below – we'd love to hear from them! They can also find out more by visiting our website.

schools@barringtonstoke.co.uk
www.barringtonstoke.co.uk

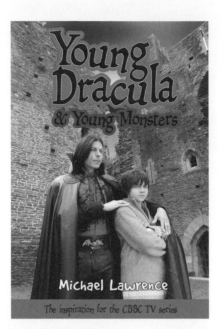

Young Dracula & Young Monsters

2 great stories in 1!

Young Dracula
Count Dracula is the nastiest vampire of them all. So how come his son is the most rubbish vampire ever? Can Young Dracula show his father what he's made of?

Young Monsters
It's Lon's first day at his new school – the Dr Ffelix Ffurter School for Young Monsters! Terrifying things stalk the corridors – and that's just the teachers! Is Lon bad enough? He'll have to be on his worst behaviour ...

You can order these books directly from our website at www.barringtonstoke.co.uk

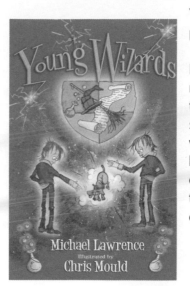

Young Wizards
by Michael Lawrence

Brin and Arlo are just two normal boys. Or so they think. But today is a very special day. A day when weird things start to happen. Things that can only get weirder when there are young wizards about ...

Ways to Trap a Yeti
by Annie Dalton

How to trap a yeti.
You will need: Ropes.
A gun. A loyal servant.
A very big box.

Watch out for: Yeti magic.

If the yeti sees you coming, you'll be the one stuck in a box ... maybe forever!
Why not trap a goldfish?
It's a lot easier!

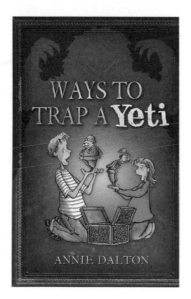

You can order these books directly from our website at
www.barringtonstoke.co.uk